Even

Andy Gutman

First published by Dog Ear Publishing
4011 Vincennes Road
Indianapolis, IN 46268
www.dogearpublishing.net

ISBN: 978-145756-456-7

This book is printed on acid-free paper.

Printed in the United States of America

Even

Early in the morning

I came to kiss you goodbye

You said please don't go...please don't go

As I walked away

I knew I couldn't stay

My head was hanging low

Even when I am not with you,
I am always there

Even when I am far away,
in my mind you'll stay

For all the times you wanted me near and
the work was more than I could bear

Even when I am not there,
I am always there

Even through the storm

Even through the rain

I'll be there

No need to feel alone

If you're in pain

I'll be there

Even when you're old

And everything's changed

I'll be there

Just listen to this song

Even when I'm gone

I'll be there

In the middle of the day

When I am working away

My mind drifts to you

Without you I am blue

And your heart knows the truth

Your heart knows the truth

Even when I am not with you,
I am always there

Even when I am far away,
in my mind you'll stay

For all the times you wanted me near and
the work was more than I could bear

Even when I am not there,
I am always there

Late in the night

I came to kiss you goodnight

You rubbed your sleepy eyes

And held on to me tight

...daddy loves you

CPSIA information can be obtained
at www.ICGtesting.com
Printed in the USA
BVHW092357200619
551589BV00001B/2/P